Shopping!

illustrated by Jess Stockham

What do we need to buy? Pasta? Catfood?

We need some more fruit. I'll make a list.

I can see the bus. Do we have any coins?

This way to the supermarket. Come on!

Shall we have a basket? No, it's too small.

Stay with me. I don't want to lose you.

I found the catfood! One box or two?

Go on, try some! I don't like this cheese!

Can you pack while I pay? Thank you!

Here come the eggs. Be careful with them!

Now let's eat. Look who's over there!

This is delicious. Can we come here again?

Why are you crying? Are you still hungry?

This medicine is for Pat next door.

I'll pay. How much are these pencils, please?

This looks great. I think I'll buy it.

These oranges are juicy! Let's buy some.

What vegetables do we need to buy here?

What shall I draw with my new pencil?

Is that my medicine? Thank you so much!

Let's fill the fruit bowl. Will it all fit in?

Where shall I put this? Where's the catfood?

What shall we draw? You choose!